Dear
Chris, Holly,
MaryKate
Have a Healthy happy year
12/29, 2003
Love Aunt Carole & Uncle Rich

Wishing You...

... fa la la la la ...

President: Jeramy Lanigan Landauer
Vice President: Becky Johnston
Managing Editor: Marlene Hemberger Heuertz
Art Director: Laurel Albright
Associate Editor: Elizabeth Clarke
Production Artist: Stewart Cott

Wishing You...

Illustrated and Written by
Sandi Gore Evans

Welcome to a winter wonderland of holiday cheer
fresh from the pen and paintbrush
of Sandi Gore Evans!

It all starts in her backyard with the first snowfall...

Like most backyards, it is a place where
miracles happen and memories are made.
Inspired by loving family,
close friends and her cozy mid-western home,
Sandi shares with you the ABCs of
holiday wit and whimsy.

She hopes you will take a moment to enjoy this book and
reflect on the simple joys of the season with...

Blessings from
Sandi Gore Evans

Wishing You...
Blessings from A to Z

The Simple Joys of the Season

...the Aroma of a warm cup of cocoa and cookies with sugar sprinkles.

8

B

...Bright shiny stars to place on top of the tree...
Beckoning to all...come, follow me.

Follow the Star.....

Cookies, Candy, and snow Cones
shared with a friend for a
very sweet day.

D⭐

...Inner peace each and every Day...one Day at a time.

E ...Evergreens, all decked out with twinkling lights...

and the drive around town to check it all out.

F

...Singing the songs of the season with Family and Friends.

...fa la la la la

...fa la la la la ...

G ...the Glee Club...God Loves each and everyone...and wants us to love one another.

And...Heaven and Nature Sing...♫

14

...Hope, within each seed is the

memory of springtimes past,
and the promise of all things new.

I...Incredible snowflakes...each one a miracle, different from the other.

© '94 Sandi Gore Evans

...Joy, Joy, Joy,
Joy down in my ♥.

...**K**nowing that good friends will always be there... ...even when my whole world is turning upside down.

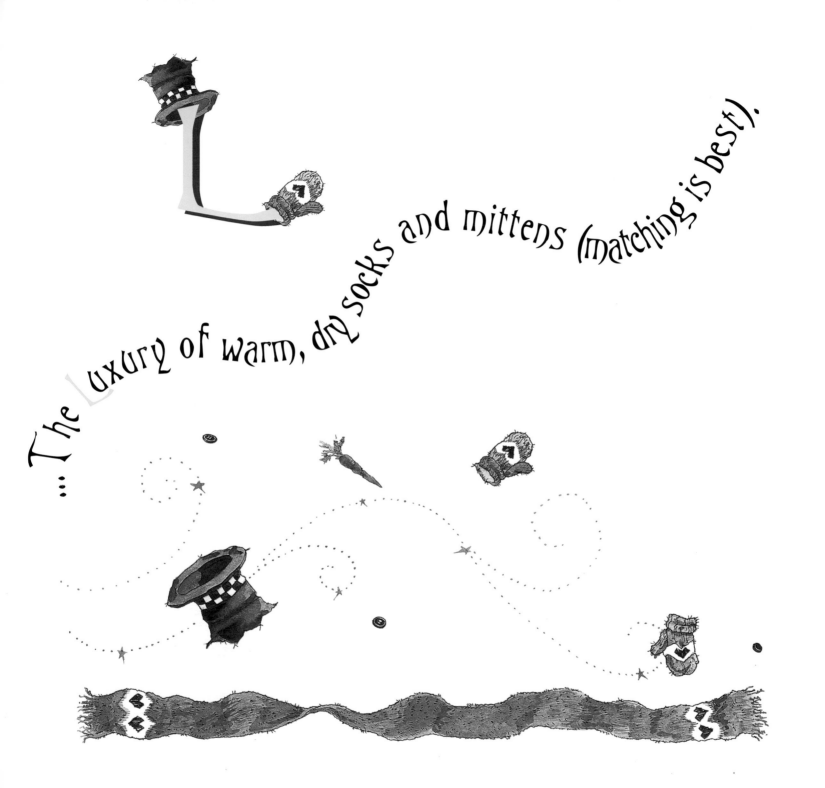

...The Luxury of warm, dry socks and mittens (matching is best).

19

M

...Roasting Marshmallows for smores

and debating whether they should be toasty brown or black.

N ...the rosey cheeks and Noses of children and tissues!

O ...Christmas Ornaments...made by little hands

Or passed down from One generation to the next.

...All of life's surprises...no Peeking!

23

Q ...Snuggling up in grandma's Quilt...

A blanket of Snow and a warm cozy quilt

and peace...and Quiet.

PEACE

R...Redbirds, and chick-a-dees and sparrows that sit on my window feeder. (If only I could fly!)

...Seed catalogues that arrive in the winter...
daydreaming on a gray - sky - day.

T...Traditions...knowing that we are a part of our forefathers and our grandchildren.

LOVE

Standing Under... the mistletoe.

Merry Kissmas

V...Little Voices that giggle with delight

when Santa has come and gone.

...Sending Warm Wishes Your Way

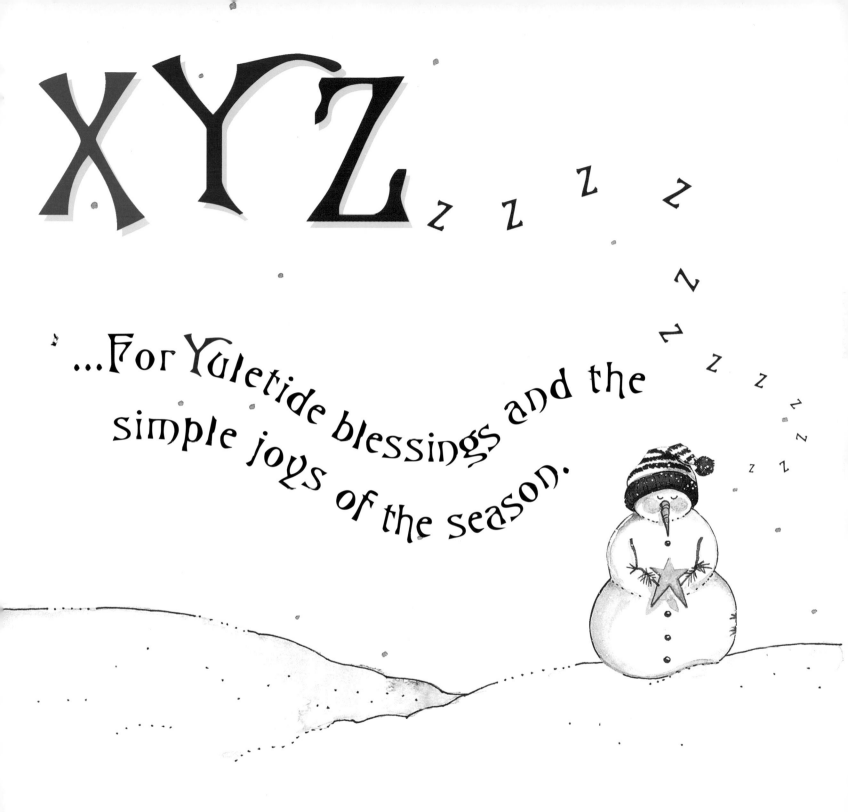

XYZ

...For Yuletide blessings and the simple joys of the season.

Wishing You...Happy Endings